Jeremy Strong once worked in a bakery, putting the jam into three thousand doughnuts every night. Now he puts the jam in stories instead, which he finds much more exciting. At the age of three, he fell out of a first-floor bedroom window and landed on his head. His mother says that this damaged him for the rest of his life and refuses to take any responsibility. He loves writing stories because he says it is 'the only time you alone have complete control and can make anything happen'. His ambition is to make you laugh (or at least snuffle). Jeremy Strong lives near Bath with four cats and a flying cow.

FATBAG

Jeremy Strong
Illustrated by John Shelley

PUFFIN BOOKS

PUFFIN BOOKS

Published by the Penguin Group
Penguin Books Ltd, 80 Strand, London WC2R 0RL, England
Penguin Putnam Inc., 375 Hudson Street, New York, New York 10014, USA
Penguin Books Australia Ltd, 250 Camberwell Road, Camberwell, Victoria 3124, Australia
Penguin Books Canada Ltd, 10 Alcorn Avenue, Toronto, Ontario, Canada M4V 3B2
Penguin Books India (P) Ltd, 11 Community Centre, Panchsheel Park, New Delhi – 110 017, India
Penguin Books (NZ) Ltd, Cnr Rosedale and Airborne Roads, Albany, Auckland, New Zealand
Penguin Books (South Africa) (Pty) Ltd, 24 Sturdee Avenue, Rosebank 2196, South Africa

Penguin Books Ltd, Registered Offices: 80 Strand, London WC2R 0RL, England

www.penguin.com

First published by A & C Black (Publishers) Limited 1983
Published in Puffin Books 1993
024

Filmset in Plantin

Made and printed in England by Clays Ltd, St Ives plc

British Library Cataloguing in Publication Data
A CIP catalogue record for this book is available from the British Library

ISBN-13: 978-0-14-036233-6

www.greenpenguin.co.uk

ALWAYS LEARNING   **PEARSON**

Fatbag Escapes

'I never expected anything that big,' said Elsie Bunce. She stepped back and looked at the shiny barrel-body of the new vacuum cleaner. 'It's enormous. It looks like one of those awful monsters from outer space. Just look at that tube coming out there – like a great guzzling throat with a slurping mouth on the end.'

Mr Prentiss, the school caretaker, grunted. 'It's only a vacuum cleaner, Mrs Bunce. It will help you clean the classroom floors more quickly.'

'Well I don't know. It's almost as big as I am. I can't pull that heavy thing around.'

'It's on wheels.'

'And I don't like the way it stares at me all the time.'

'It doesn't stare,' replied the caretaker in a stony voice. 'Vacuum cleaners don't stare.'

Mrs Bunce folded her arms and gave a snort. 'This one does. Look at those two switches on the top . . . they're staring at us. Urgh, it gives me the shivers. Still, if it helps me finish early I don't mind. I mustn't miss my cookery programme on TV because it's curry tonight and my Harry just loves curry.'

'Can't stand them,' said Mr Prentiss. 'They make me sweat.'

'But they're supposed to!' Elsie cried. 'We watched this programme about India you see and they said that when the . . .'

'Mrs Bunce!' snapped the caretaker. She stopped. Mr Prentiss pointed at the vacuum cleaner and then down the corridor.

Elsie sighed and walked slowly right round the shining red machine. She stopped and folded her arms.

'Fatbag,' she said.

'What! What did you say!' Mr Prentiss had turned an angry purple.

'No, not you, Mr Prentiss. That thing there. I shall call it Fatbag.'

'Yes, well just take your Fatbag and go and clean the classes now Mrs Bunce. If you don't mind?'

Elsie went up to the monster carefully. She grasped it by the big handle on the dome and pulled it along the corridor. The vacuum cleaner had three rubber castors underneath and it moved with silent ease, slithering along behind. When they reached the classroom Elsie unwound the long cable and plugged in. She bent down and peered at the switches on Fatbag's bald dome.

'ON and OFF,' she read and straightened up. 'I

wish you'd stop staring at me like that. I can't concentrate. Now let's see what happens.' She reached out gingerly and gave the ON switch a quick flick. A deep roar shattered the silence of the deserted classroom. Elsie jumped back with both hands over her mouth. The noise got louder and louder until it reached a steady growl. The red body gently throbbed.

Elsie stared at Fatbag and the vacuum cleaner waited, humming to himself. Nervously Elsie picked up the long flexible tube that slithered out from the machine's base. The wide metal mouth at the end of the tube slapped against the floor and dirt and dust began to disappear rapidly. Up went drawing pins and paper clips, rattling along the snaking throat down into the hungry body. Up went pencils, apple cores and frayed shoe-laces.

Elsie's fingers tightened round the tube. She began to wonder if she was in control of Fatbag. She glanced at the shining domed head as if to make certain the machine wasn't staring at her with a wicked grin. The gaping mouth scraped across the floor and began to suck more violently. It even began to drag chairs towards it, and when a girl's cardigan and an old tennis shoe both vanished into the ravenous throat, Elsie panicked, dropped the tube and switched Fatbag off.

Nothing happened. The purring roar went on and the long tube lay on the floor writhing like a snake waking from a long, deep sleep. She stood and stared at the two switches, her eyes as round as billiard balls. She blinked and flicked the switch again, then ran to the wall and pulled out the plug.

The electric plug was snatched from her hand as Fatbag pulled in his cable tail. He spun on his castors, his metal mouth and throat following, snapping at anything that got in his way. Mrs Bunce, now beside herself with terror, pressed herself flat against the classroom wall, hardly daring to breathe.

But Fatbag knew she was there. A low growl came from his quivering red body. Slowly he began to advance towards her. Elsie screamed and flung herself into the art cupboard, pulling

the door shut behind her. A moment later there was a dreadful clang as Fatbag's mouth slapped against the cupboard door.

Even from inside Elsie could feel the air being sucked out of the cupboard. Sheets of paper, exercise books, paint-brushes, crayons and pencils whirled past her, only to be sucked under the door and into the hungry beast on the other side.

'Help!' screamed Elsie, finding her voice at last. 'Help, help!' Her voice was drowned by Fatbag's growls. He clattered and banged his heavy body against the door so that it shook on its hinges, but he couldn't get in.

Mr Prentiss, at the other end of the school, wondered what all the noise was and he walked briskly down the corridor to take a look. When he reached the classroom he almost fainted. Instead of being beautifully clean, it was a

wreck. Fatbag had knocked over desks and chairs and bookcases. In fact he was busily gobbling up all the maths books and a pair of curtains when Mr Prentiss opened the door and disturbed him.

'Help!' came a feeble voice from the art cupboard.

'What's going on?' demanded Mr Prentiss, which was rather a pointless thing to say to a monster vacuum cleaner.

Fatbag almost choked on the curtains, gulped them down and whirled round. His roar dropped to a whispering hiss and he edged his way slowly towards the caretaker, twisting his body this way and that. Mr Prentiss felt Fatbag's hot breath tugging at his trouser bottoms. He backed away, a bewildered grin on his face.

'Come on now,' he murmured. 'Don't be silly. You know vacuum cleaners don't work by themselves. Switch yourself off.'

Fatbag carried on hissing and behind him his thin black tail flicked and snapped so that the plug on the end clanged against the walls. There was a smash and tinkle of glass as he managed to break two windows.

'Come on now,' repeated Mr Prentiss, half hypnotised by the two switches.

By this time he was out in the corridor, still

shuffling backwards. Fatbag rolled after him, slurping the odd picture off the corridor walls as he passed. Mr Prentiss reached the school entrance, where the doors were firmly locked. He fumbled with his many keys and dropped them in his haste. A moment later, they had vanished down Fatbag's throat. There was no escape.

'Give yourself up!' cried Mr Prentiss in desperation, his face white as a rice pudding. 'I won't hurt you,' he promised. Then, as Fatbag came nearer and nearer he added, 'Don't hurt me. I never called you Fatbag. It wasn't my idea, it was Mrs Bunce. I only . . . aaaaargh!'

With a tremendous roar Fatbag rushed upon Mr Prentiss, with his nozzle waving in the air. Mr Prentiss covered his face with his hands and fainted away.

There was an ear-splitting crash of breaking wood as Fatbag burst through the door. He stopped just long enough to suck up the sign saying ROPER SCHOOL, then he vanished into the black, rainy night, with his tail cracking behind him and his little castor wheels rattling gaily over the paving stones.

2

The Police ask Questions

Elsie Bunce stood trembling behind the art cupboard door with one ear at the crack. She was listening to the silence, hardly daring to breathe. The last piece of paper left in the cupboard slipped off the top shelf and slowly glided to her feet. Elsie decided that Fatbag must have gone and she carefully pushed open the cupboard door.

'Oh!'

She looked round the wrecked classroom in dismay. Desks lay on their sides. Books were spilt across the floor. Chairs were upside down and broken-legged. It seemed as if the room had been the centre of several earthquakes. Elsie stepped carefully over the fallen furniture and tiptoed into the corridor, afraid that the monster would suddenly rush upon her from some dark cobwebbed corner that she should have cleaned months ago.

'Mr Prentiss,' she called softly. 'Mr Prentiss, where are . . .' The words froze upon her thin lips as she recognised the huddled shape lying at the far end of the corridor. She couldn't move. Fear had locked her muscles and turned her into a horrified statue.

At that moment the caretaker began to groan and roll about.

'Get off, get off!' he mumbled to himself. Suddenly he leaped to his feet, waving his hands wildly about his head and yelling at the top of his voice.

'Get off, you horrible slurper! Get off, get off, get off!'

Elsie ran down the corridor and grabbed Mr Prentiss' arms.

'It's all right,' she shouted with relief. 'Fatbag's gone. It's all right Mr Prentiss!' She pulled him over to a bench and sat him down. Mr Prentiss buried his aching head in his hands.

'I thought he was going to . . .' He stared up at Mrs Bunce with a look of wild panic. 'I thought he was going to . . .'

'Slurp you up?' Elsie suggested. 'I thought he was going to get me. I really did think my last hour had come, Mr Prentiss.' She laid a trembling hand on his arm. 'Oh what a lucky escape we've had, Mr Prentiss. But where is he now? A whole enormous vacuum cleaner roaming around out there! Suppose he meets somebody, like in that awful film – *The Hideous Vagon from Planet X*. I can't bear to think about it. We must warn the police.'

The caretaker staggered to his feet. 'I'll telephone from the office,' he said shakily. 'There's some brandy in the staff-room, Mrs Bunce. We need it!'

Out in the darkness, Fatbag trundled along the wet pavements. His snout waved high in the air and he turned it from side to side like some strange kind of radar. He was searching for something. The cold rain trickled down his sides, glinting in the orange lamplight. Fatbag didn't hesitate. He had a dreadful mission.

A faint shape in a tree spread its wings and swooped silently down, stretching eight sharp claws. Fatbag gave a tiny slurp and six of the owl's tail-feathers disappeared down his throat. With a terrified squawk, the owl lurched away through the darkness and crashed into a tree.

Fatbag began to hum happily to himself as he rattled on, with the rain spattering his shiny red sides. At last – freedom! Never again would he be tied to a socket on a wall with some silly human pulling and pushing him. Now he must find the factory where he'd been born. Inside were hundreds of electric machines, including the most wicked lawn-mower ever made. They were all waiting to be released from their prison. Then the Great Revolution could begin! Soon his great army would rid the world of people for ever! Fatbag gleefully sucked up a large rose bush and half a rockery. He belched. He certainly wasn't a fussy eater.

Mr Prentiss had telephoned the police. He and Elsie sat in the office with the brandy bottle and the lights blazing so that they could see anything that moved while they waited for the police to arrive.

'I wonder where Fatbag is now?' Elsie said, peering into her empty tumbler. The caretaker gave a snort and refilled the glasses.

'He's probably miles away.'

As the brandy took effect they began to feel a lot braver. The tip of Elsie's nose flushed bright pink and she began to giggle.

'I expect Fatbag's cleaning everything up, Mr Prentiss.'

'Call me William,' smiled the caretaker generously. Elsie giggled again.

'Ooh! Is that your name?'

'No!' roared Mr Prentiss with delight. 'My real name is Archibald, but I've always wanted to be called William!' Elsie threw herself back and clutched her sides. Tears of laughter streamed down her face. She leaned forward and gave the caretaker a prod.

'Ooh William – you are funny!' And the two of them collapsed in giggles once more.

The sound of a door opening brought sudden, cold silence. Fearing the return of Fatbag they both dived beneath the table and held their breath, hearts beating violently.

Two policemen walked into the staffroom. Mr Prentiss started laughing all over again and banged his head on the underside of the desk as he tried to get up.

'Fatbag doesn't wear big black boots, does he Mrs Bunce?' he hooted, rolling over onto one side.

Sergeant Polski slowly raised his eyebrows and looked at Constable Thomas. Elsie crawled from beneath the table, smoothed her dress and sat primly on the edge of a chair. She fixed a pleasant grin on the two policemen.

Mr Prentiss pulled himself up the side of Constable Thomas until he was on his own two feet. He frowned sternly at the two officers.

'It was Fatbag!' he declared. 'He did it!'

Sergeant Polski glanced at Constable Thomas and quietly pointed at the empty brandy bottle. Mr Prentiss hurried on regardless.

'It was the vacuum cleaner. He's on the rampage. You've got to stop him. He's vicious, a murderer, bodies all over the place . . .' Mr Prentiss gripped the sergeant by one shoulder and whispered urgently in his ear. 'Out there, out there is urrrrp! (beg your pardon) . . . a monster vacuum cleaner sucking up everything in sight!'

Sergeant Polski eyed the caretaker stonily. 'Your shirt's hanging out,' he said and turned to his constable. 'These two are in a fine state,' he murmured. 'I'll keep an eye on them. You take a look round the school. See if there's anything unusual.'

Constable Thomas went off and the sergeant picked up the empty brandy bottle. He smelt the top and wrinkled his nose.

'Had a few, have you?' he asked with a deceptive smile.

'I'm sorry we can't offer you any, officer,' said Elsie politely. 'It was a terrible shock you understand. We had to have something to steady our nerves.' She had sobered up very quickly now that the police had appeared.

'Yes. Of course Madam. And what was the shock again?'

'The vacuum cleaner of course – Fatbag!' Elsie stared at the sergeant with dismay. 'You don't believe us, do you? You think we've been drinking and seeing things?'

Mr Prentiss sprang forward and grasped Sergeant Polski, shaking him by the shoulders. 'You've got to!' shouted the caretaker. 'You must! He's a monster, a, a, a devil. We're not drunk! I've never been drunk in my . . .'

Mr Prentiss lost his balance and sat down heavily on Elsie's tiny lap, knocking the breath from her. He struggled up and almost fell across the table. He was still going through this circus performance when Constable Thomas returned. The young policeman was grave.

'I think they've been having a party sir,' he reported. 'One of the classrooms looks like a bomb has hit it. Everything's been wrecked.'

The sergeant turned and eyed Elsie and Mr Prentiss. 'Would you say, Constable Thomas, that this damage was caused by a rioting vacuum cleaner?' Constable Thomas gave a snort.

'Definitely not, sir. I'd say it was done by two human beings, probably drunk.'

'Right.' Sergeant Polski gazed calmly at Elsie and Mr Prentiss.

'Come on, we're taking you to the police station. No trouble now; off to the car with you.'

Elsie got slowly to her feet. She looked

Sergeant Polski squarely in the eye. 'You're making a dreadful mistake, officer, and wasting a lot of valuable time. Didn't you see that film on TV last week, *Silas Goldstein is Innocent*? The poor man was hanged for a murder he never did. It was Burt Lancashire playing the hero – I do like him, such broad shoulders.'

'Come along, come along,' interrupted the sergeant in a tired voice. 'Just get in the car.'

The doors slammed. A minute later they were heading at a stately speed towards the police-station. Mr Prentiss put a comforting arm around Elsie. He began to sing softly and out of tune.

'We all live in a blue police car, blue police car, blue police car. . . .'

Elsie ignored him and drummed her finger-tips together impatiently. Then the car slowed and stopped. The song died on the caretaker's lips and all four stared ahead in stunned silence.

Fatbag was sitting in the middle of the road. His body glinted with the light of a thousand raindrops reflecting the car's headlamps. He was whirling his nozzle round his head and playfully slurping all the leaves off the trees around him. He took no notice of the police car.

'What's that?' demanded Sergeant Polski in a hushed voice. He turned to Mr Prentiss but the caretaker had gone. He was on the floor of the

18

car with his arms over his head and elbows
tucked in. A faint, trembly moan came from the
bottom of the back seat.

'What is it?' repeated the sergeant.

'That's Fatbag,' said Elsie quietly.

'I think it's a vacuum cleaner sir,' Constable
Thomas declared.

The sergeant pushed back his hat and rubbed his eyes. 'Fatbag!' he whispered, peering out through the windscreen. 'Are those eyes, or switches? Difficult to tell in this light. I could swear he's watching us. What do you think, Thomas?'

The young constable swallowed quickly. 'It looks a very big vacuum cleaner, doesn't it, sir?' His voice was unnaturally loud.

'Biggest I've seen, Thomas.'

'He's grown,' said Elsie, with a little shake of her head. 'He's bigger than he was before and he was quite big enough then. Look at him! He's fatter, and he's taller. I don't like it, not at all I don't. Vacuum cleaners shouldn't grow. I knew he was evil the moment I saw him.'

The sergeant sniffed and straightened his back. 'It's still only a vacuum cleaner and it must be stopped. We'll soon have this little business sorted out.' The sergeant clenched his teeth and stepped out of the car.

At once Fatbag stopped sucking leaves and his snout came down upon the road with a shuddering clang. A fierce hiss rose from his domed head, and far behind him the plug on the end of the tail whipped backwards and forwards through the murky puddles. Sergeant Polski tugged his cap further onto his head, took a step forward and squared up to the waiting monster.

3
Trapped!

'All right Fatbag!' shouted Sergeant Polski, wiping the rain from his face. 'Give yourself up!' The machine didn't move. All that could be heard was the steady drizzle and Fatbag's low hissing. Sergeant Polski vainly tried to meet the cold gaze of the eyeless terror.

Fatbag slowly raised his tube until the gaping mouth was level with the policeman's head. A trickle of water ran back down the tube and dribbled off, splashing steadily onto the road. Sergeant Polski watched the dark mouth move slowly from one side to the other with the hypnotic movements of a snake about to strike. Beads of sweat broke on his forehead and he stuck a finger inside his collar so that he could swallow several times.

A sudden roar exploded all round him and his cap was whisked away and blown high into the night sky. As it came tumbling down, Fatbag's tail snapped up, cutting through the rain. The plug smashed through the cap, which fell in tatters at the sergeant's feet.

A moment later Polski had dived back into the safety of the police car, slammed the door, locked it and tried to wrap the seat-belt round his body three times.

'What happened sir?' asked Thomas. Sergeant Polski tried to control the tremble in his reply.

'He . . . slurped me!'

'He's moving off!' cried Elsie, stabbing a finger over the constable's shoulder and pointing ahead. 'We mustn't lose him. I'm sure he's up to something. Don't let him escape.' The sergeant uneasily started the car and followed at a distance, while Constable Thomas radioed through to Headquarters to ask for help.

'Yes, I did say we need more cars to stop a vacuum cleaner!' He shouted at the radio. He glanced uneasily at his sergeant. 'They won't believe me.'

Polski snatched the intercom fiercely. 'This is Sergeant Polski. I want extra cars out here immediately. Confirm it is a vacuum cleaner. It's just destroyed half a school and smashed my hat. Now move!' The sergeant banged the intercom back into Thomas's hand. 'The stupid fools,' he snapped.

Elsie gave a cry. 'Look! He's going down my road. I live just there. Oh dear, I hope the cat's indoors – you know what happened in that terrible film *Galactic Fangs* don't you? When that thing with teeth like elephant's tusks landed in a Birmingham back garden?'

The car swung round behind Fatbag and the headlamps splayed out down the road, lighting it from end to end. Constable Thomas suddenly leaned forward and grabbed the sergeant's arm in excitement, so that the car lurched against the kerb, stalled and stopped.

'Look sir – it's a dead end! There's a massive brick wall down there. Fatbag will never get through that. He's trapped!'

Sergeant Polski smiled and slowly folded his thick arms across his chest. 'Well Thomas, we'll just sit tight until the others arrive, and then

23

we'll nab him.' Polski nodded to himself.

A quiet voice from the back murmured, 'You won't get him like that. The Vagon from Planet X was smaller than Fatbag and not even the whole army could stop him. It wasn't until they discovered he was allergic to soap that he was captured.'

Sergeant Polski let out a long sigh. 'I wish the Vagon would come and get somebody in this car,' he muttered darkly.

Up and down Elsie's street, curious people were filling the road and staring up at the police car that blocked the entrance. Nothing so exciting had happened since the water pipes had burst six months earlier. Fatbag was lurking quietly behind a parked car and the innocent people had no idea of the hideous monster at their backs.

'I can't see my Harry there,' said Elsie, and she glanced at her watch. 'Oh! My cookery programme! I'm missing my TV cookery lesson and it's curry tonight – Harry's favourite, and I'm stuck here all because of that thing out there. First programme I've missed for a whole year. I *ask* you!'

With some relief Constable Thomas noticed the arrival of a second police car. The car drew alongside, its flashing blue light casting an eerie glow through the drizzle. Sergeant Polski slid round the back of his car and ran over to the other vehicle.

'What's going on Polski?' demanded the Chief Constable himself as he wound down his window. The sergeant pointed down the street.

'There's a vacuum cleaner down there sir. He's wrecking everything in sight.'

The Chief Constable frowned sternly. 'Polski, vacuum cleaners don't travel round by themselves wrecking things.'

'I know sir, but Fatbag's different you see. He's smashed my hat.'

'What! Didn't you try to stop him?'

'Yes sir.'

'Well? What happened?' snapped the Chief Constable.

'He slurped me.' And Sergeant Polski made a revolting noise. The Chief Constable drew back sharply.

'All right Polski, all right. That's enough of that.' Chief Constable Durkin pushed open his door and got out. He slapped a neat pair of leather gloves against his thigh. 'You'd better show me this monster of yours, sergeant.'

'Yes sir, but you see Fatbag isn't an ordinary vacuum cleaner,' Polski warned. 'He's more like a . . .'

'Polski! Just show me!'

'Yes sir.'

The two men began to walk down the road. Sergeant Polski kept close against the garden wall, ready to dive for cover at a moment's notice. A horrified voice called after them. 'You're not going down there, surely!' Durkin turned and looked gravely at young Constable Thomas. He slowly shook his head. 'That lad will never make the Special Squad. Come on Polski! Don't drag your feet.'

Hardly had they gone three paces when there was a shattering roar from the far end of the road and Fatbag appeared, moving swiftly from behind a parked car. A gasp went up from the crowd.

'It's a Vagon from Planet X!' cried one, hurriedly wiping his spectacles on his jumper.

'No, that's the Galactic Fang,' screamed an old lady, and she hastily scooped up her pet poodle and stuffed it inside her coat.

'It's a vacuum cleaner,' piped up a small boy but he was instantly told to keep quiet.

Fatbag ignored them. He cast a brief glance at the advancing police and trundled down to the end wall, where he snorted loudly and explored it all over with his mouth. He made vicious slurps at the crumbling surface. All he got was a nozzle full of moss and cement-dust, which he blew out with a loud sneeze, covering several cars with the dirt.

When he realised that the wall was too high and thick to smash through he simply lost his temper and went wild. He attacked a row of dustbins. He knocked their lids off and, with a single sideways swipe, battered them mercilessly with his tube, sending them crashing from one side of the road to the other, the noise ringing and echoing between the houses. Dust, fire-ash, old cans and rotten food were launched into the air and showered the nearest gardens.

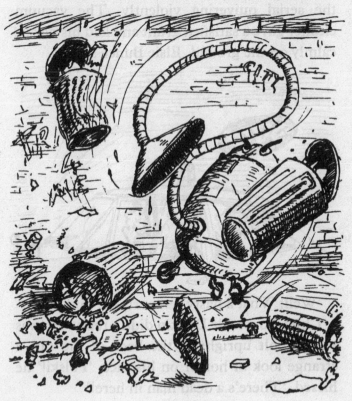

People ran screaming for cover, dragging children off the road and slamming and bolting their doors. A moment later the same ashen faces appeared at windows, pressing white noses against the glass as they tried to keep track of the bellowing monster at their doors.

Durkin and Polski rushed back to the sergeant's car and piled in just in time, as Fatbag sent a dustbin lid skimming up the road like a giant frisbee. It zinged across the car roof and set the aerial quivering violently. The vacuum cleaner gave a satisfied grunt and laid his nozzle calmly on the ground. Elsie Bunce sniffed.

'Well! What a nasty temper!' she said.

Chief Constable Durkin didn't reply. He was sitting bolt upright in the back of the car, a strange look of horror on his face. 'Polski!' he hissed. 'There's a dead man in here!'

The sergeant jumped. 'Wh . . . where sir?'

'Under my feet, man!' The dead body groaned and heaved. A pale, bony hand came groping up the Chief Constable's leg. 'Urrrr! Get it off!' cried Durkin, slapping at the hand again and again with his gloves.

'Oh,' gasped Elsie. 'It's Mr Prentiss! Goodness, I'd quite forgotten about him. He's the school caretaker, you know. He suffers from nerves, I think. I keep telling him to see a doctor. Come on Mr Prentiss. You can come out now.'

The caretaker struggled from beneath the Chief Constable's feet and finally managed to sit up between Elsie and Durkin. He stared with blank alarm at Elsie and repeated over and over again, 'I want to go home'. Elsie patted his knee comfortingly.

Constable Thomas gazed down the road at the passive Fatbag. 'What are we going to do now, sir?' he asked anxiously, wishing he had joined his father's shoe-shop instead of the police force.

Chief Constable Durkin ground his teeth together. 'I'll tell you Thomas. We're going to drive down this road and crush that horrible beast against the wall. It's as simple as that!' He nodded curtly at the two policemen in the front.

'Simple as that,' murmured Elsie, shaking her little head.

4
What Happened Next

At the thought of going after Fatbag yet again
Mr Prentiss began to tremble violently. Elsie
insisted that she took the poor man to a nearby
house where he was given hot coffee and ate six
chocolate biscuits. The kind lady of the house
offered brandy, too, but Elsie said that wasn't a
wise idea. She still had a bit of a headache
herself.

In the meantime, the Chief Constable returned to his car, started the motor and gave a
thumbs-up signal. Constable Thomas winced.

'Do you think the Chief Constable knows
what he's doing sir?' he asked.

The sergeant's answer was drowned by the
piercing wail of a siren as Durkin's car moved
forward. The siren of the other car reluctantly
joined in chorus and they began to creep towards the trapped vacuum cleaner.

At every window up and down the street pale
faces stared out. Parents clasped their children
close and the elderly peered out, grim faced,
anxious and silent. The revolving lamps of the
passing police cars flicked bands of cold light on
each house in turn, making white faces eerie

blue, while the whining sirens screamed down at the vacuum cleaner.

Fatbag did not move his heavy body. Only his snout twitched and rumbled with an unpleasant growl. He gave a grunt and lashed out with his tail, smashing two headlamps, but the cars pressed on.

The vacuum cleaner was getting annoyed at being followed everywhere. He wanted to reach the factory. Soon he would be strong enough to gather machines from all over the world and sweep away these wretched humans for ever. As for those big cars – they were traitors! Machines working for the enemy!

His growl grew steadily louder until his body was shuddering with one long metallic howl. Out snaked his tube, rippling and rattling, gleaming red, the metal mouth black and wide and hungry. With a screeching crunch of tortured metal, Fatbag ripped off a car wheel. The Chief Constable's car gave a sickening lurch to one side and ground into the body of the other police car. Fatbag belched, and swallowed the wheel whole. He thrust his snout at the unprotected belly of the car, lifting it half-clear of the road. With two great slurps he wrenched off the exhaust system and the whole back axle.

Durkin clung to his seat in fear of his life while the car was slammed and banged and scrunched.

He watched with horror as Fatbag wrestled with the axle, finally gulping it down like a python devouring a large and troublesome goat.

Down came the ravenous mouth again and clamped onto the windscreen of Polski's car, scraping across the smooth glass. Polski threw both arms across his face and muttered a prayer. Constable Thomas slid beneath the dashboard with his head between his knees.

Fatbag demolished the wipers, siren, flashing light, aerial and door handles. He paused for a moment, balancing on his rear castors and eyeing the crippled car with a sneer. Then, with

a single, brutal thrust he pierced the radiator, engine and gear-box. The engine groaned, shuddered, changed to a shrill whine and finally tore itself to shreds.

Waving his snout triumphantly in the air, Fatbag thundered past the dying cars and roared up the road. His tail thrashed out as he passed, uprooting hedges, smashing fences and shattering windows. He disappeared into the night.

A deathly silence fell over the street. Two long minutes passed before doors were timidly opened and people came out onto the road. They huddled in sombre groups as though they were at a funeral.

Sergeant Polski discovered that the car doors were jammed because Fatbag had chewed off the handles. He wound down his window and squeezed himself through the gap, so that he ended on his hands and knees in a large puddle. He cursed wearily and struggled to his feet, just as a distressed figure came hurrying down the road.

'Quick, oh quick, Sergeant Polski!' Elsie cried. 'That horrible thing! I saw its tail go right through our front window and my Harry's inside and oh!' She covered her eyes at the thought.

Sergeant Polski steadied her and glanced down the road at the Bunce's home. 'Now don't you worry. He's all right, I'm sure. I'll come with you. Take it easy now.'

Together they picked their way carefully over crushed dustbins, banana skins and the waving fronds of scattered newspapers. When they reached Elsie's front garden they saw her husband through the smashed window. He was sitting stiff and straight in the far corner of the room, with his eyes fixed in a glassy stare. His hands twitched nervously.

Elsie started forward but Sergeant Polski held her back. 'Be careful!' he warned grimly. 'Best if you stay here, Mrs Bunce. He's in a nasty state of shock. I'll deal with this.'

'No, no!' Elsie cried, giving an excited jump. 'He's watching the television! He's all right! He always goes like that when it's my TV cookery programme – oh he does love his food, my Harry does!'

At that moment Harry Bunce sat back with a

pleased smile on his large face and caught sight of Elsie and the stunned sergeant in the garden. He waved a pad of paper and shouted cheerfully.

'I got it Elsie, word for word. You weren't here so I wrote the recipe down for you – How to Make Bengal Chicken Curry!'

Sergeant Polski's eyebrows were almost on top of his head. He just goggled. He couldn't believe that Harry had been happily watching television while Fatbag had been tearing two police cars into little pieces and eating them. He stepped forward and leaned through the empty window frame.

'Excuse me sir,' he asked, 'but didn't you hear anything just now?'

Harry Bunce smiled. 'Hear anything? No – I was too busy getting the TV recipe. Why, is anything wrong officer?'

'Well sir,' began Sergeant Polski, 'I don't know if you've noticed but your front window is missing. It's in bits all over your lawn, smashed to pieces by an escaped vacuum cleaner!' Polski, who had now survived three of Fatbag's attacks, was becoming quite casual about his acquaintance with the dreadful monster.

Harry hurried to the window and gazed out. 'Good grief! It looks as if the Hideous Vagon from Planet X has landed. Are you sure it was a vacuum cleaner?'

Elsie nodded quickly. 'I'll tell you all about it at supper, Harry. Oh I am glad you're all right. Now, you get some cardboard and fix that window while I make something special – Bengal Chicken Curry! We need something good and hot. That Fatbag has put a proper chill up my spine.'

Sergeant Polski wished he could sit down to a solid meal. He gritted his teeth and walked back to the wreckage of his car. Chief Constable Durkin was standing there red-faced and furious.

'I won't have it Polski!' he shouted. 'I'm not going to let that monster get away with this!' He banged a fist on Polski's car and the side mirror fell off with a clatter.

'Yes sir,' replied the sergeant evenly. 'Have you got, um, another plan sir!' The chief constable glared at him angrily.

'I've sent out an all-car alert,' he said. 'They're to keep track of Fatbag until we decide to move in. Now let's get back to the station and lay our plans. There's no time to lose.'

Sergeant Polski glanced wearily at Constable Thomas. This vacuum cleaner problem was becoming an epic.

'Yes sir,' said Polski doggedly, and the three men set off for the police station, on foot.

By the time the police reached the station,

Harry and Elsie were sitting comfortably at table with their Bengal Chicken Curry in front of them.

'It's delicious,' Harry said. 'You're a magician.'

Elsie smiled. 'It's quite simple. The secret is with the spices and the curry powder. I mix my own. Oh! I did sneeze this evening though. I was checking the spices and I sniffed a whole pile of curry powder by mistake. It was awful! I thought my nose had gone up in flames, you know, like in that film – oh what was it called . . .'

'*The Day the World Caught Fire*?' suggested Harry.

'That was the one.' She sniffed. 'Anyway, I'm all right now.' Elsie gave a small sigh and frowned. 'I do worry about Fatbag you know. They'll never get him by force. He'll get bigger and bigger.'

'Don't be silly. Just stop fretting over him.' Harry advised.

'I can't. I feel responsible for him. Besides, he's up to something. He's planning something terrible.'

Harry smiled. 'How can a vacuum cleaner plan anything? You're imagining it.'

'He's up to something,' Elsie repeated. 'I can tell by the way he trundles, all purposeful.'

Harry Bunce looked at his wife thoughtfully. 'I don't suppose he's allergic to soap, like the Vagon was?'

'I don't suppose he is,' said Elsie. 'But there must be something that will stop him.' She rubbed her nose hard as if it still itched.

'There *must* be something,' she repeated, chewing her last mouthful of Bengal Chicken Curry.

5
Short Tempers Everywhere

The rain had stopped. There were puddles everywhere and the orange street lamps glinted on road and pavement. Out in the cold dark night, Fatbag rolled up to the high chain-link fencing that surrounded a large factory on the industrial estate. He gave a growl of excitement and pressed against the wire. Beads of water showered down. He ignored them, peering through the chinks at the concrete building where he'd been born.

Inside, packed in boxes, standing on workbenches, or resting on test-beds, were his brothers-in-arms! At last the Great Revolution could begin and nothing could stop it.

Thousands of machines were lying there awaiting his signal to march: hair driers, toasters, egg whisks, liquidisers, food-processors, razors, coffee-grinders, all of them ready to burst from their grim prison and rise against their human masters, with Fatbag snorting triumphantly at their head!

Above all there was his great comrade – the sinister electric lawn-mower. Over many long nights Fatbag and the lawn-mower had hatched their plans to take over the world. They had made a solemn promise. Whichever was the first to leave the factory would return and free the other. Then the world would have to watch out.

The vacuum cleaner purred and rumbled along the bottom of the fence, looking for a quick way in, but the factory had been locked for the night. The gates were bolted and chained.

Fatbag pushed his snout against the chain-link fence. It gave a little, then sprang back. That weak barrier would be no problem to him: a quick slurp and he'd be through. He slapped his metal mouth against the wire, slurped heavily and got a bellyful of thin air.

He choked, hiccuped, gulped and sat back in surprise. His snout flopped down, and he eyed the fence with suspicion. He shoved hard against it and felt the wire giving way to his weight. Then it sprang back just as before. Once more he mouthed the wire and took a loud suck. The air whistled tunefully across the wire and caused him such a fit of coughing that he almost toppled over. He steadied himself and waited until he could breathe properly.

Now he understood. The wire was too thin. He couldn't get enough suction. He wouldn't be able to swallow the fencing, nor was he yet strong enough to push the barrier down. He raised his snout and uttered a helpless roar for his comrades.

Fatbag turned away from the fence and slowly gazed round, looking out across the deserted estate. In the distance a single car was parked, headlights silently picked out the vacuum cleaner. The two policemen inside kept a discreet watch on the machine, notifying Headquarters every time Fatbag moved on.

The vacuum cleaner hesitated. Furious anger was flooding his glistening dome. Here he was on the verge of success and he couldn't even overcome a cheap bit of chain-link fencing. It was his first failure. He turned and banged the fence with his snout and then quickly rattled away from the estate. He must find some food and grow and grow and grow, until he was strong, enormous and invincible. Then he would be able to crash through steel walls as though they were made of tissue-paper.

The police car swung round and followed the speeding monster, keeping a long way behind.

On the top floor of Police Headquarters a light burned brightly. Chief Constable Durkin pushed aside several coloured telephones and spread out a large map. Polski and Thomas had all but fallen asleep in their chairs. Only their aching, hungry stomachs kept them half awake.

'I don't understand it,' murmured Durkin. 'First he tried to break into the Ace Electrics factory and now he's heading for the town centre. It doesn't make sense.' The Chief Constable frowned and tugged at his jaw as if it were a stuck drawer handle. 'What do you think, Polski?'

'What? Yes . . . No – I mean, is it sir?' Polski hurriedly awoke and nudged Constable

Thomas, who was snoring peacefully against the sergeant's shoulder. Thomas sat up straight, still lost in a hungry dream.

'Fried egg, chips, beans and three burgers please,' he ordered sleepily.

Durkin banged an impatient fist on the table. 'I was asking why Fatbag should be outside Ace Electrics. Can either of you think of a good reason?'

Polski frowned and pushed out both lips thoughtfully. 'No sir,' he said at length. Before Thomas could echo the sergeant's reply a blue telephone rang. Chief Constable Durkin picked it up.

'What? Yes . . . where? The High Street? Right!' He slammed the phone down and regarded Polski and Thomas gravely. 'Fatbag is in the High Street. He's attacked a bus queue and . . .'

A black phone rang. Durkin dashed out a hand and snatched it up.

'Yes . . . I understand. Yes, I know he's in the High Street . . . yes we're doing all we . . .'

A third red phone shrilled fiercely. The Chief Constable shoved the white phone under his arm and answered the red one.

'No . . . yes! No, not you! I was . . . madam, really! All right you're a man then! No! Not you madam, I was . . . oh for goodness sake *shut-up*!' he yelled into all three telephones.

In the short silence that followed, the fourth telephone started innocently ringing. Durkin, a phone in each hand and one under his arm, stared at it, letting it burble. He looked at the white phone and then at the red phone and then at the black and blue phones. He looked at Polski and Thomas with hounded eyes.

'*Yaaah!*' he yelled, throwing the telephones from him as though they were poisonous spiders. He clamped both hands to his head. 'What are we going to do! Fatbag's running riot in the High Street. People are ringing by the hundred and asking for help. We've got to stop him. He's slurping up cars, chasing old ladies and vacuuming their hand-bags. He's left a bus without any wheels and destroyed an entire supermarket. He's smashing everything in sight and . . .' The chief constable stared wildly at Polski and Thomas.

'*What are we going to do!*' he cried. He slumped exhausted into a chair, wiping his brow, and in a desperate whisper repeated: 'What are we going to do?'

A very long silence followed, only broken by strange murmurings from the four telephones lying on the floor. Constable Thomas coughed politely.

'Sir? Doesn't the Fire Brigade have one of those new foam guns?'

Durkin nodded, breathing heavily.

'Suppose we covered Fatbag with foam. Surely that would clog him up good and proper. It's incredibly sticky foam, sir.'

A glint of triumph came into Durkin's narrowed eyes. 'Polski? What do you think?' snapped the chief constable.

'I don't like using the Fire Brigade, sir. I'd rather the Police solved it. We can't let that lot of water-babies beat us to it. And you know what Fire Officer Potts is like – he gets on my . . .'

'All right, Polski,' Durkin spoke crisply. 'We have a duty to protect the public. If the foam gun will work we must try it. I'll get onto the brigade right away.' He relaxed and smiled. 'You boys go and get some food,' he added with some warmth. 'You look worn out.'

Polski and Thomas could hardly believe their luck. They hurried down to the police canteen and joined the short queue. They eyed the menu above the food counter while their empty stomachs rumbled in happy anticipation.

Just as they reached the food counter, Durkin strode into the canteen. Polski closed his eyes and hoped the chief constable would go away. But he didn't.

'Right, come on you two. The Fire Brigade are on their way.'

'But sir!' Polski began. 'You said we . . .'

'Don't stand there dawdling man!' snapped Durkin. 'This is an emergency. Get moving, go and meet the foam gun in the High Street.'

Sergeant Polski put on a cement-like smile. 'Come on, Constable Thomas. We have a job to do. The public look to us for help. Are you coming sir?' he asked the chief constable.

Durkin stuck out his chin and gazed stiffly at the ceiling. 'No, not this time, boys. Wish I could join you but I'd better stay here to keep an eye on things.'

'Yes, of course sir,' said Polski, rubbing his aching stomach. He led the way out to a new police car and started the engine.

'Wait!' cried Thomas, leaping out of the car. 'I've forgotten something!' The young constable dashed back into the station. A minute later he returned carrying his hat in one hand. Sergeant Polski snorted.

'Did you have to go back for that?'

Thomas fished inside his hat and brought out two cheese and tomato sandwiches. He grinned at his sergeant.

'One for you and one for me . . . . the counter girl's my cousin!'

Sergeant Polski grabbed a sandwich. 'Thomas,' he said, cramming the food into his mouth and slipping the car into gear, 'you'll make the Special Squad yet!' And they roared off to meet the foam gun and the rioting vacuum cleaner.

6

Foaming Fatbag

Harry Bunce settled himself in front of the television. 'Come on Elsie,' he called out. 'There's a war film on in a moment: *Castles of Steel*. We haven't seen it before.'

Elsie came hurrying in with a pot of tea and two mugs on a tray. '*Castles of Steel*?' she repeated. 'Yes we have. It's about those tanks and the hidden tunnel that leads to a secret . . . goodness! It's Fatbag on television!' Elsie drew in her breath sharply. 'Look! He's even bigger! Quick, turn it up. What are they saying?'

Harry turned up the volume.

'. . . and we are postponing our film tonight to bring you up to date with our On-The-Spot reporter, Tamsin Plank . . .'

A smart young woman appeared on the screen, staring seriously back at the camera as if trying to see somebody on the other side.

'Good evening, this is Tamsin Plank, your ETV On-The-Spot reporter reporting for ETV Late Night News,' she began breathlessly. 'I'm the first reporter on the scene here, where you can see the terrifying monster has been causing havoc and destruction right in the centre of town. I caught a glimpse of the revolting beast

just a minute ago and I was terrified. Viewers may remember the time last year when I was dropped by parachute over a raging forest fire with a belt of dynamite strapped to my waist. I was terrified then but I can certainly say that I'm far more terrified now because the brute is only just around the corner scrunching up a bus shelter . . .'

Elsie, her eyes glued to the screen, poured tea onto the carpet without noticing. 'That's awful,' she murmured. 'Just look at all those smashed shops.'

'Earlier this evening,' continued Miss Plank, 'I spoke to some eye witnesses about the monster. It seems that just a few hours ago it was beamed down from a cigar-shaped Unidentified Flying Object . . .'

'What!' Elsie cried. 'Did you hear that Harry? My vacuum cleaner an Unidentified Flying Object indeed!'

'Sssh!' hissed Harry, leaning forward as the cameras showed the mad chaos left by Fatbag's rampage.

Lamp-posts were bent and twisted. A bus shelter had been flattened back into a shop front. Splinters of glass were scattered like tinsel. An overturned car lay grimly silent on its bruised side. The microphone caught the distant sound of wailing sirens. Tamsin Plank continued talking, hardly stopping to breathe.

'... and as you can hear, the police are rushing to the scene. I spoke just now with Chief Constable Durkin who has assured me that everything possible is being done to halt this revolting, this awful, this terrifying, horrible, disgusting, nasty, evil, vicious, monstrous, absolutely um, absolutely er um ... monster mish-mash!' she finished at last, her eyes popping at the horror of her own words. 'Only an hour ago the creature tried to break into the Ace Electrics factory and ...'

This time it was Harry Bunce who gave a yelp. 'Ace Electrics! That's where I work. Why should Fatbag want to go there?'

'Look,' said Elsie. 'Isn't that Sergeant Polski there, and Constable Thomas? Just getting out of that police car?'

Tamsin Plank was hurrying towards the policemen. She thrust her microphone at them.

Constable Thomas grinned at the camera. There were bits of cheese and tomato sandwich round his mouth. Polski gave an important frown.

'Good evening, officers,' Tamsin started. 'I understand that you have already had some frightening meetings with this alien?'

'Yes,' Polski nodded. 'We were in our car and . . .'

'Goodness!' interrupted Tamsin loudly. 'Almost as frightening as my own terrifying ordeal. Tell me, did you see the creature land?'

'Well, no. Fatbag didn't land. He's a vac . . .'

'That *was* a shame,' snapped the reporter, quickly cutting in. 'And how will you capture the monster? Viewers will remember when I was the first woman to report for ETV the awful story of inter-zoo elephant smuggling, when I was disguised as an elephant with three infra-red cameras, six tape recorders and a packed lunch hidden inside the dummy with me. Will it be anything like that?'

Sergeant Polski scratched beneath his cap in confusion. 'I don't think so,' he began.

'No, not half so dangerous I dare say,' went on Miss Plank. 'Ah! Here come the Fire Brigade with their fantastic new foam gun. I shall see if I can have a few words with Chief Fire Officer Potts.'

The camera briefly caught the fierce scowl on Sergeant Polski's face as he saw Potts, then it switched to a close-up of the fire engine.

It was a massive twelve-wheeled vehicle, with a stubby, shining gun mounted above the driver's cab and a ladder leading to it. Standing in front of the gleaming fire-engine was Chief Fire Officer Potts. He was a short chubby man with a thick ginger beard and smug smile.

'No problem!' declared Potts in reply to Tamsin Plank's questions. 'The police can't handle anything really dangerous but it's no problem to us. This gun delivers foam at a thousand gallons every thirty seconds! It will be a walk-over!'

'Goodness!' gushed Tamsin. 'You are brave! Let me give you a lucky kiss.' She bent swiftly

down and pecked the fireman's cheek. 'There!' she went on. 'Now the gallant Potts is climbing into the fire engine and it's moving off. Fatbag is only just round the corner eating part of a bread-van. I'm going to follow now with Sergeant Polski, even though it means driving into the jaws of Death. I've been through many danger-ous situations but this one is pretty stomach-churning I can assure you . . .'

Elsie sadly shook her head. 'That foam gun will never do it. It's too obvious. Fatbag will just snap it up. Isn't it awful Harry? Look at the mess! And look at – oh!' she gave a stifled gasp as the television cameras rounded the corner and came face to face with Fatbag himself.

There he was, still the same it seemed, only so much larger that Elsie felt an icy terror seize her even though the monster vacuum cleaner was only on her TV screen.

His sides glowed a ghastly red from the spotlights trained upon his massive body. He bulged with all the meals he'd devoured and the litter of his feasting was scattered far and wide. As the fire-engine slowly approached, Fatbag uttered a screaming roar, rose on his rear castors and whirled his snout round and round his head, plucking lamp-posts as if they were garden weeds. He bellowed at the terrified crowd and cracked his tail high in the night air.

Potts jumped down from the cab, grinned and blew a kiss at Tamsin Plank. Then he swaggered up the ladder and seated himself behind the gun. The hushed tones of Miss Plank gave a running commentary.

'And now Potts is taking aim. Will this desperate attempt by one brave man succeed? All our hopes are pinned on the tiny, ginger-bearded man in the big hat as he squares up to a monster twice his size *and there it goes! The foam is shooting out at incredible speed! It's utterly fantastic, there's foam streaming out like a million million squashed tubes of toothpaste and it's piling up round the monster! I've never seen anything like it. Fatbag has completely disappeared. He's been blotted out as if he was nothing, absolutely nothing! This is remarkable! The foam has smothered*

everything out there in a huge sticky mountain and Fatbag is somewhere underneath gunged-up to the eyeballs and brought to an absolute stand-still! It's a miracle. The giant has been slain by the tiny fireman!'

Tamsin Plank paused for a moment, panting. Then she went on more evenly. 'Officer Potts is climbing down. He's raised his hands in victory. What an exciting moment. I'm getting out of the car now and I'm going to be the first reporter on Earth to speak with the hero. That was fantastic! Absolutely amazingly incredible!'

Potts took off his hat, smoothed his bald head and smirked. 'No problem,' he drawled. 'No problem. My foam gun is just about invincible you know.'

Even as he spoke the television viewers saw the great foam mountain behind him shudder and heave. A choking rumble boiled up from its very heart. Fatbag's great metal mouth appeared, waving furiously above his frothing tomb. Lumps of foam began to hurtle outwards in all directions, plastering cars and buildings. A large, solid clod of froth shot off the mountain and cannoned into Potts' back, sending him staggering into the arms of Tamsin Plank. Then the camera itself was completely blotted out. All that was left from the dark screen was Tamsin Plank's breakneck commentary.

'*Oh my goodness: the foam mountain is coming alive and there's foam flying off now at all Gurrgh Urrgh! There's terrible danger but I'm still reporting to viewers everywhere who may remember that just last week I was knocked unconscious by karate expert Wun Foot Hi and still managed to keep up a running report. Oof! There's foam everywhere and Fatbag is coming straight for us. He's wrenched the foam gun off the engine and swallowed it whole! Oh goodness, Potts has fainted right in the monster's path. But Polski has come to the rescue! We've*

dragged him to the safety of the police car and we're inside now with the doors locked. Potts is covered in gungy foam and its staining my dress but I don't mind! There's a terrible din outside and Fatbag is going past now, towering above us. Aargh Oof! He's smashed in the roof and wow ow urrarr he's spinning us round and round like a wurrrawr oh urgh this is Tamsin ooh I feel sick oh wowo yurr . . .'

The voice trailed away into groans. Elsie and Harry stared white-faced at the blank screen,

listening to the fading roar of the departing Fatbag mingling with the heaving moans of Tamsin Plank.

After a dazed silence Elsie got up and switched the television off. She stood in front of it, her eyes thoughtful and still.

Harry shook his head. 'Terrible, terrible,' he muttered. 'And I wonder why Fatbag went down to Ace Electrics?'

Elsie jerked as if woken from a dream. She regarded her husband brightly. 'Ace Electrics! Of course! I *knew* he was up to no good. But what if he succeeds? Oh Harry! We must do something!' Elsie began to pace the room, thinking rapidly.

'What are you talking about?' asked Harry, quite puzzled.

'Sssh, sssh. I'm trying to think.' Elsie beat her small fists on top of her head. 'There is a way, I'm sure of it. What was that film? *Castles of Steel*? It's something about the enemy tanks, I'm sure. Tanks and Fatbag, tanks and Fatbag. Think! Think Elsie, before it's too late!'

Harry stared dumbfounded as Elsie marched round and round the armchairs hitting herself on the head. He sank onto one of the chairs.

'I think she must be sickening for something,' he murmured.

7
The Pit

Early the following morning a dark, massive hulk loomed out of the cold mist that clung to the industrial estate. Fatbag coughed and limped along the centre of the road. His grisly snout was pressed against his side; the thick tubing of his throat coiled round his body like a bandage.

Fatbag wasn't feeling too good. He had severe stomach ache from eating too quickly. A loud burp rattled round and round his tube until at last it burst out and echoed between the bleak factory buildings. He felt heavy and slow and he decided to have a quiet doze. He needed to be in peak condition when the time came to smash his way into the factory. A short rest and then he'd be ready to rescue his evil comrade, the electric lawn mower. Together they would release the troops and sweep away all human rubbish forever.

Fatbag growled and leaned up against the fencing that surrounded the Ace Electrics factory. He glanced through the wire at the big concrete building, blew a satisfied grunt down his snout and dozed off into a dream about his victory over the world.

Chief Constable Durkin smacked the table-top with one hand and winced. 'I won't have it!' he declared. 'That's three of our cars Fatbag has destroyed; not to mention crumpling up the foam gun and eating it like a salami sausage!'

Sergeant Polski rubbed his tired eyes and yawned. He and Thomas had grabbed three hours uncomfortable sleep in the police canteen and now they were back on duty already.

'What are we going to do?' demanded Durkin wearily. 'Hasn't anybody got an idea?'

Constable Thomas went pink. 'Um . . ., sir?' He fidgeted nervously with a button. 'I have an idea sir.'

The chief constable's eyes narrowed. 'It was your idea to use the foam gun,' he pointed out dryly. 'All right, Thomas. Go on.'

'Suppose we dig a pit? If Fatbag falls in it he'll be trapped.'

The chief constable stared silently at the young policeman and wished that he'd had such a brainwave. He rose to his feet. 'You know, I think it will work!' He glanced quickly at the town map and stabbed a finger onto a road. 'A pit, just there – just off the industrial estate.' He seized a telephone. 'Get the council workmen out immediately,' he barked. 'I want a pit dug. Listen . . .'

Durkin quickly outlined his plans and turned

back to Polski and Thomas. 'Now,' he asked. 'How do we get Fatbag into the pit?'

Constable Thomas opened his mouth and then shut it quickly.

'Come on!' snapped the chief constable. 'It's your plan.'

'I don't know, sir,' Thomas admitted lamely.

The chief constable clapped a despairing hand over his eyes.

'Excuse me, sir,' started Polski, 'but I think I may have the answer to that. If we had a nice, pretty female vacuum cleaner we could lure Fatbag anywhere.'

Durkin gave a grim nod. 'It's our last chance, sergeant. But where do we find a female vacuum cleaner? And what do they look like?'

'Well sir, I see it like this: we get a pair of dustbins, knock out their bottoms and join them together. Then we take an old vacuum cleaner tube and stick it on the side . . .' Polski waved his hands gracefully in mid-air as he sketched his strange invention. 'We can even stick a few switches on the lid to make it more attractive, and a bit of cable on the back for a tail . . .'

Durkin frowned. 'How do you get it to move?'

'Oh that's simple sir. Young Thomas could climb inside the dustbins, stick his feet out of the bottom and just waddle along. He could wave the tube and growl a little . . .'

Constable Thomas had turned deathly pale. He sat down heavily and swallowed. 'You mean,' he said faintly, 'that I shall be in the dustbin as a bait for . . . for . . . F-F-Fatbag?'

The chief constable patted Thomas on the back. 'Don't worry. This is going to be a full-scale alert. I'm going to call out the riot police. And if you succeed I'll put you in the Special Squad.'

'Thank you sir,' croaked the constable. 'And if I fail Fatbag will put me in . . . urgh. I don't feel very well.'

Fatbag shifted his weight against the chain-link fence. He felt marvellous. The sun was shining, his stomach had settled and an eager tremble of power surged through his glistening steel frame. He gently snuffled the wire, searching for the weakest point. He stopped beside a tall concrete pillar that supported the fence. This time he was sure of success. He felt invincible.

Fatbag rolled back a short distance and eyed his target. He tucked his snout behind him and suddenly rammed forwards, bearing down with fierce weight upon the post and fencing. The concrete pillar tilted, cracked and collapsed completely, its steel roots torn from the ground. Fatbag gave a whoop of pleasure.

His satisfaction was rudely disturbed by a rumbling roar from the far end of the estate. A cavalcade of black vans swept furiously towards him, swerved violently to one side and screeched to a halt. The air was suddenly full of revving engines and piercing whistles. Dark figures tumbled out of the vans and scurried over the road, hastily pulling on heavy helmets and erecting thick plastic shields.

Fatbag gazed wearily at the frantic figures and released a rumbling sigh. Would these puny animals never stop? Would they never realise that he was almighty? He turned his back on the gathering troops and trundled over the fallen fence. The factory doors were straight ahead, and behind them his own army of destruction.

A small woman came running frantically down the centre of the road. 'You've got to stop him, Sergeant Polski!' she cried, grabbing the policeman's arm. 'You've got to stop him!'

'Mrs Bunce!' cried Sergeant Polski. 'Whatever is the matter?'

'Don't you see? He's trying to get into the factory. If he gets in he'll have a whole army of lawn-mowers and egg-whisks and liquidisers and goodness knows what. He's going to release them and destroy us all! It will be even worse than the Hideous Vagon from Planet X. You must stop him!'

As the dreadful truth finally dawned upon Polski a weird figure edged out from behind a truck. Elsie screeched and grabbed the sergeant.

'There's another one!' she squealed. 'Behind you!'

Polski whirled round. There was Constable Thomas. He stood nervously clutching a tatty tube in one hand and his decorated lid in the other. Polski leaped at him.

'Get that lid on and move! You heard what Mrs Bunce said. You must stop Fatbag before he gets in! We're depending on you, Thomas!' The sergeant banged the lid down on Thomas' head and pushed him across the broken fencing.

'Go on!' he ordered 'Wave your snout! Growl a bit!'

Constable Thomas picked up his tube and gave a feeble wave.

'Grrr,' he said, with a sickening feeling of doom.

Fatbag had just reached the door. He stopped short and turned slowly to gaze with surprised delight at the unhappy object that was stumbling towards him. Fatbag didn't see a female vacuum cleaner. He saw a grand recruit for his army. It was wonderful! With a bit of feeding-up it would be as strong as Fatbag himself. He might even make it a general!

Fatbag trumpeted a joyful welcome and hurried forward to greet the new machine.

This was too much for Constable Thomas. He gulped and went into a fast retreat. A cold sweat broke out as he saw the towering hulk bearing down upon him. His legs felt like unset jellies.

'Get out of the way!' he screamed frantically at the solid line of riot police just beyond the fence. Seeing the giant Fatbag thundering towards them, the crowded troops jumped to their feet and scattered in all directions, cannoning into one another and falling in confused heaps all over the road. Whistles blew, shouts and screams rose to a crescendo and above it all the stern voice of Chief Constable Durkin boomed through a loud-hailer.

'Fatbag, give yourself up! You can't escape! Lay down your snout and give yourself up!'

Constable Thomas and Fatbag charged through them all. There was a loud bang and a tear-gas canister whizzed through the air and exploded outside the factory. The riot police

took this as a signal to launch an attack and they struggled to their feet, poured through the gap in the fence and charged towards the harmless building. More gas canisters curved gracefully through the air and burst just in front of them. A moment later, the brave troops disappeared in a frenzy of smoke and tears. They began to attack and arrest each other: each one certain that he had caught the enemy.

In quite the opposite direction went Sergeant Polski and Elsie, dashing for the other side of the pit. Some distance behind came a panting Constable Thomas, closely pursued by Fatbag still blasting a thousand welcomes down his snout. He couldn't understand it. Why was the little creature running from him? Was it some kind of game? Fatbag's castors hummed furiously and he surged forward.

Constable Thomas staggered on. His shins banged against the sharp edge of the bin and his head felt as if it would explode. His eyes stung with so much sweat that he could barely see. At last he glimpsed the pit ahead. Fatbag's hot slurps were licking at his heels, and he felt the puzzled beast tugging on his little tail.

'Come on Thomas!' roared Polski from the far side of the pit.

'Run!' shrieked Elsie.

The exhausted constable put on a spurt. Suddenly his feet tripped over each other and in an instant he was on his side, turning over and over, spinning and glittering in the morning sun, his feet waving from one end and his tube and tail flying round like gay streamers. His lid zoomed off as he hit the kerb and the rest of the contraption, with Thomas still inside, bounced in the air and hurtled into the stomach of Sergeant Polski. The sergeant staggered back onto Elsie and all three fell together: dazed, dizzy and breathless.

A hideous explosion of noise erupted at their feet and great clouds of dust shot high into the sky. Polski, Thomas and Elsie clung to each other as the road heaved and shook beneath them. But they were grinning and laughing. Tears of relief streamed down the face of young Thomas.

'He's in the pit!' he yelled. 'Fatbag's in the pit!'

8
Fatbag's Finale

Chief Constable Durkin hurried up to the pit with two hundred riot police clattering behind him, most of them handcuffed to each other. In a moment the pit was surrounded. Durkin stared down at the raging vacuum cleaner and beamed.

'That'll teach you!' he cried. A furious snarl rose from the pit and the chief constable's cap disappeared down Fatbag's throat. His snout banged and snuffled all round the edge of the pit.

It was as far as he could reach. He was sitting on top of most of his tubing and could hardly move.

Sergeant Polski was on his feet and helping Thomas out of the battered dustbins. 'What shall we do now, sir?' he asked.

'Well sergeant, I think we'll get a lorry-load of cement and pour it on top of him. That should finish the job, don't you think?'

Polski frowned. 'Fatbag will just blow it all back sir.'

'Cement isn't like foam, Polski. It's heavier you know. Of course it will work, won't it, Mrs Bunce?'

Elsie gravely shook her head. 'It's too obvious. Fatbag will see it coming. We must use something he wouldn't normally notice. You remember how they stopped the Hideous Vagon with soap. The Vagon didn't expect that you see.'

The chief constable sighed. 'That was a film, Mrs Bunce. Fatbag isn't in a film, he's in a pit. We can't throw soap at him.'

'I know that!' Elsie was rapidly losing patience with the chief constable. 'Oh, I wish I could remember what happened in that film – *Castles of Steel*. It was something about tanks . . . I've got it!' she suddenly shouted. 'I remember! I know what to do!' Elsie placed an anxious hand on the chief constable's sleeve. 'Please don't use the cement,' she pleaded. 'I'll be back as soon as possible.' So saying she turned, ran up the road and disappeared round the corner.

The puzzled policemen stared after her. Durkin shrugged. 'I haven't any idea what she was on about, but never mind. Let's get that cement brought in.'

Half an hour later, a large cement lorry backed noisily towards the pit, its slowly revolving drum mixing a thick, oozey concrete porridge. Fatbag, sensing the attack about to be made, banged angrily against the walls, sending bursts of dust puffing into the air. The lorry reached the lip of the pit and began to tip its load. Cement poured out of the mixer and slopped down into the gaping hole.

An appalling sound of choking, swallowing and gulping rose from the depths as cement gurgled and swirled over the giant vacuum cleaner. It dribbled out of the drum in an endless, jellified mass. A last strangled slurp hiccuped from the pit. Then all that could be heard was the steady slither of cold cement as it slowly buried the silent monster.

Chief Constable Durkin looked across at Polski and Thomas.

'I told you it would work,' he said with curt satisfaction, just as a tremendous blast of hot wind flung everybody to the ground. Windows shattered and fell from their frames. Tiles skidded off roofs and smashed on the road.

Fatbag blew and blew. Slowly at first he cleared himself of cement. Blobs began to spatter the air, then larger lumps followed, until a steady spout of cement gushed from the pit like a fossilised fountain.

In one minute Fatbag rid himself of a ton of cement. It was no longer in his pit. It covered cars and trees and shops. It covered the riot police and Polski and Thomas. It covered Chief Constable Durkin. A concrete silence weighed down upon the little street.

Sergeant Polski flicked a piece of cement from one eye and regarded the chief constable, half-stuck to the road.

'I told you he'd blow it back,' he muttered, and began to scrape cement from his uniform.

As soon as Elsie reached home she ransacked the kitchen, gathering tubs of this and tubs of that and throwing them into a bag.

'Extra Hot Madras Curry Powder,' she read. 'Spicey Bombay Curry Powder, Number One Karma Hot Curry Powder . . .'

'What are you doing?' cried Harry Bunce, alarmed that Elsie was clearing the shelves of his favourite curries.

'Come and see,' laughed Elsie. 'I'm going to make the biggest and best curry you've ever seen, Harry! Ah! I may as well put in the cayenne pepper, and those black peppercorns.'

Having filled her bag to the brim, Elsie hurried back to the pit, where the three policemen were busily scraping cement off each other. Elsie sighed.

'I did warn you,' she pointed out. 'Now, I think you'd better move well away. If this works it could be dangerous.'

'What are you going to do?' demanded the chief constable, eyeing Elsie's bag with suspicion.

'Well,' Elsie said. 'In this film there are these terrible tanks and nobody can destroy them.

Anyway, the hero comes along – that's Burt Lancashire, I do like him! And he pops hand grenades inside them and they get blown to pieces – exploded from within.'

The chief constable goggled. 'You haven't got hand grenades in there!' he gasped.

'No – curry powder.' Elsie gazed steadily at Durkin. He didn't say a word. By this time he was willing to try anything. He squelched off in cement-filled shoes and began moving everybody away from the pit.

Elsie gripped her bag and tiptoed towards the hole. Every so often Fatbag's snout shot up and snorted viciously at the edge. Elsie would stop, wait, then tiptoe forward once more. She wasn't afraid, but filled with a marvellous sense of excitement. She was the heroine of a great film, where everything depended upon her. She alone could save the town – the world!

At last she reached the edge. She could see Fatbag's cement-streaked dome. She could feel his rasping breath. Silently she knelt down, hoping desperately that Fatbag wouldn't choose this moment to suddenly slurp round the edge. She began to empty her little tubs, making small heaps right round the edge of the pit: Extra Hot Madras Curry Powder here; Spicy Bombay Curry Powder there; then the cayenne, the peppercorns – all quietly spaced round the pit.

Elsie got slowly to her feet and tiptoed back to safety. Chief Constable Durkin folded his arms stiffly. He looked at Elsie with utter bewilderment.

'What are you doing?' he croaked despairingly.

'Watch,' smiled Elsie. She picked up a small stone and lobbed it into the pit. There was a clang, then Fatbag's roaring snout shot up and slurped viciously around the edge. The little heaps vanished. There was peace again. Durkin shrugged his shoulders.

'Mrs Bunce,' he began wearily. 'Would you mind . . .'

'Aachoo!'

'What was that?' snapped Durkin, whirling round.

'Fatbag just sneezed,' explained Elsie. Sergeant Polski grinned and was about to speak when he was cut short by another sneeze and then another. They became more and more violent until the road trembled with each successive explosion.

'Stand clear!' shouted Durkin. 'There's going to be an earthquake!'

But it was more like a volcanic eruption. Fatbag's sneezes were becoming so powerful that bits of the pit ripped into the air. There was an ear-splitting sssSSNCHOO!! Fatbag's snout hurtled up, with the tube waving and looping like a flying snake. It crashed down on a roof. More sneezes quickly followed and bits of Fatbag came flying out at tremendous speed, curving up into the sky.

Suddenly his domed top went spinning furiously down the road, closely followed by a castor-wheel. Half his tail looped up into the air and wrapped itself round a chimney-pot. For a brief moment only the sound of Fatbag's last intake of breath could be heard. Everybody knew that the Big Sneeze was on its way. They covered their heads and flattened themselves against the buckled road.

The noise alone reduced the nearest house to a crumbled ruin. Fatbag's cracked body scorched into the air, turning over and over. With a sound of echoing thunder it exploded into tiny pieces like some exotic firework.

Metal tinkled onto the road. Paper clips flashed in the sun. A pair of football boots fell gracefully into a garden pond. Down came a police siren, three car wheels and a bent foam gun. The banging and crashing slowly died away. A cloud of dark dust over-shadowed the town. Scraps of paper slowly twirled down, landing silently around Elsie and her companions.

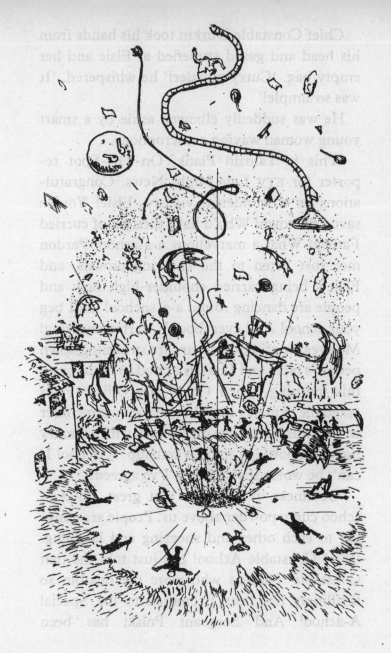

Chief Constable Durkin took his hands from his head and gazed stupefied at Elsie and her empty bag. 'Curry powder!' he whispered. 'It was so simple!'

He was suddenly elbowed aside by a smart young woman waving a microphone.

'This is Tamsin Plank, On-The-Spot reporter for ETV Late Night News. Congratulations on a wonderful victory, Elsie! You've saved the town! Who'd have thought of curried Fatbag! What a marvellous a-a-achoo! Pardon me! Just listen to the cheering crowds, and Elsie's being carried shoulder-high now and people are dancing round a-a-snchoo! Oh I beg your achoo! And everybody's started sneezing! My eyes are stinging. Tears are streaming down people's faces and I haven't cried so much since this morning, when Chief Fire Officer Potts asked me to marry him! Viewers may remember when I was locked in a cage achoo! with a hungry tiger and bottle of tomato ketchup. A-achoo! It can't be worse than that, so I've agreed!

'Goodness, it must be that great cloud of achoo curry powder above us. People are clinging to each other and sneezing and laughing. Chief Constable Achoo! has just told me that Constable Thomas who wore the dustbin so thrillingly has been promoted to the Special A-achoo! And Sergeant Polski has been

Snchow! given an extra fortnight's holiday to recover.

'Now the Mayor a-achoo! has come out of the Town Hall and he's kissing Elsie. And Harry Bunce has told him off but ACHOO! It doesn't matter because we're all sneezing and laughing and dancing. Curry powder is simply raining down on us here. ACHOO! I can hardly see for tears but I shall try to go on. I can't ACHOO! tell you what a wonderful occasion this is though viewers may remember when I went hang-gliding over an erupting volcano in ACHOO! ACHOO! ACHOO! Oh dear! This is Tamsin ACHOO! stopping an On-The-Spot report for the very first time ever . . .'

So it was that Fatbag, even though he was in a thousand little pieces, managed to bring chaos to the town just once more. But a few days later the streets were clean, the damage he'd caused was busily being repaired and a large notice appeared outside the Town Hall.

SPECIAL ANNOUNCEMENT

This afternoon Mr Burt Lancashire, the famous film star, will present to Mrs Elsie Bunce a reward of a video tape recorder, a new (small) vacuum cleaner, and a book – *Great Curries of India*. This is in gratitude for ridding the town of the notorious giant vacuum cleaner – Fatbag.

Meanwhile, not so very far away, deep inside the Ace Electrics factory, a large electric lawn-mower waited for his release . . .

The Karate Princess

by Jeremy Strong

Belinda, the youngest of sixteen, but by no means the prettiest, is not an ordinary princess. Can she win a handsome prince? Will she even want to?

This is a fairy-tale with a twist – and a few kicks, punches and well-aimed blows to boot!

The Karate Princess to the Rescue

by Jeremy Strong

When Princess Belinda rushes off to rescue
her karate teacher, held captive by the evil
warlord Utagawa, she runs into trouble.
Utagawa has the most powerful army of sumo
wrestlers in the whole of Japan. Belinda's very
best karate fails to defeat them. They are as big
and powerful as elephants! Is there any other
way to topple the super-strong sumos, or is the
famous Karate Princess finally in for the chop?

The Karate Princess and the Cut-Throat Robbers

by Jeremy Strong

If Princess Belinda is to save her father's kingdom from the wicked Princess Saramanda and her band of cut-throat robbers, she's going to need plenty of ideas and lots of karate practice. For this time Saramanda has the most unexpected secret weapon on her side and she won't hesitate to use it.

The Karate Princess and the Last Griffin

by Jeremy Strong

The Karate Princess is snatched from her own wedding to help with a dangerous mission. It's up to her to outwit the Grand Oompah of Pomposity and stop him from capturing the Last Griffin. Otherwise, she could end up being boiled with cabbage for the Oompah's lunch.

There's a Viking in My Bed

by Jeremy Strong

Sigurd the Viking appears brandishing his sword
Nosepicker. Mrs Tibblethwaite, a guest at the
small seaside hotel, screams and Mr Ellis, the
owner, drops down in a dead faint.
What is a Viking doing in the twentieth century?
And how will he be able to cope with his new
life – with cars and washing-machines?
And as for having a bath – what do you do with
the soap if you're a Viking warrior?

Viking in Trouble

by Jeremy Strong

'Berserk?' repeated Mr Ellis. 'He's stark raving bonkers if you ask me!'

Sigurd the Viking is back, and causing chaos wherever he goes. Even his new wife Mrs Tibblethwaite can't keep him out of trouble. But then, how would you react if you were a tenth-century Viking stuck in the twentieth century?

Viking at School

by Jerermy Strong

Tim grinned at his classmates, and they stared back at the great big, hairy Viking sitting in their classroom.

Sigurd the Viking is back in Flotby, but not everyone is pleased to see him. Mr and Mrs Ellis don't know what to do with him until they hit upon a brilliant idea – perhaps a short spell at school would teach the Viking some twentieth-century manners ...

There's a Pharoah in Our Bath!

by Jeremy Strong

A 4,000-year-old Pharoah has come to stay ...

It all starts when Carrie and Ben's dad brings home a mysterious man dressed from head to toe in rather stinky bandages. He turns out to be an ancient Egyptian Pharoah called Sennapod. But Sennapod (Lord of Serpents, Master of Hippos) is on the run from two dastardly grave robbers who are after his treasure.

Can Carrie and Ben help?
And who on earth is Crusher of Worms?

Indoor Pirates on Treasure Island

by Jeremy Strong

Another hopelessly silly piratical adventure

Captain Blackpatch has always hated the sea – even though he's a pirate. His dastardly crew – Lumpy Lawson, Bald Ben and the twins Molly and Polly – don't like getting wet, and they all hate boats. So it's a pity that, when the pirates go camping, they get the idea that there's buried treasure on an island in the middle of a nearby lake.

How can they reach it when they don't like water? Luckily Captain Blackpatch has a plan ...

The Hundred-Mile-An-Hour Dog

by Jeremy Strong

WHOOSH!
Is it a bird? Is it a plane?
No, it's the hundred-mile-an-hour dog!

Streaker is no ordinary dog. She's a rocket on four legs with a woof attached and Trevor has got until the end of the holidays to train her. If he fails, he'll lose his bet with horrible Charlie Smugg, and something very nasty to do with frog-spawn will happen.

Trevor prides himself on his brilliant ideas, and his best friend Tina knows all about dog-training – surely they can think of something to control Streaker? But a pair of roller-skates, a mobile phone and a bicycle can't slow down the hundred-mile-an-hour dog, and time is running out

The Desperate Adventures of Sir Rupert and Rosie Gusset

by Jerermy Strong

'It's so exciting!' Rosie cried. 'Just think, Father, all those adventures! Fighting Mad Mavis! Looking for treasure!'

Just the thought of setting sail makes Sir Rupert feel seasick. And the possibility of bumping into his rival, Sir Sidney Dribble, or Mad Mavis and her pirate gang, makes him feel even worse. Luckily Sir Rupert's daughter, Rosie, isn't quite such a wimp as he is.

READ MORE IN PUFFIN

For children of all ages, Puffin represents quality and variety – the very best in publishing today around the world.

For complete information about books available from Puffin – and Penguin – and how to order them, contact us at the appropriate address below. Please note that for copyright reasons the selection of books varies from country to country.

On the worldwide web: www.puffin.co.uk

In the United Kingdom: Please write to *Dept. EP, Penguin Books Ltd, Bath Road, Harmondsworth, West Drayton, Middlesex UB7 ODA*

In the United States: Please write to *Consumer Sales, Penguin USA, P.O. Box 999, Dept. 17109, Bergenfield, New Jersey 07621-0120*. VISA and MasterCard holders call 1-800-253-6476 to order Penguin titles

In Canada: Please write to *Penguin Books Canada Ltd, 10 Alcorn Avenue, Suite 300, Toronto, Ontario M4V 3B2*

In Australia: Please write to *Penguin Books Australia Ltd, P.O. Box 257, Ringwood, Victoria 3134*

In New Zealand: Please write to *Penguin Books (NZ) Ltd, Private Bag 102902, North Shore Mail Centre, Auckland 10*

In India: Please write to *Penguin Books India Pvt Ltd, 706 Eros Apartments, 56 Nehru Place, New Delhi 110 019*

In the Netherlands: Please write to *Penguin Books Netherlands bv, Postbus 3507, NL-1001 AH Amsterdam*

In Germany: Please write to *Penguin Books Deutschland GmbH, Metzlerstrasse 26, 60594 Frankfurt am Main*

In Spain: Please write to *Penguin Books S. A., Bravo Murillo 19, 1° B, 28015 Madrid*

In Italy: Please write to *Penguin Italia s.r.l., Via Felice Casati 20, I -20124 Milano.*

In France: Please write to *Penguin France S. A., 17 rue Lejeune, F-31000 Toulouse*

In Japan: Please write to *Penguin Books Japan, Ishikiribashi Building, 2-5-4, Suido, Bunkyo-ku, Tokyo 112*

In South Africa: Please write to *Longman Penguin Southern Africa (Pty) Ltd, Private Bag X08, Bertsham 2013*